Horses

A Level Two Reader

By Cynthia Klingel and Robert B. Noyed

The
Child's
World®

Horses are large animals with four strong legs. They make a "na-a-a-y" sound.

Horses have long necks and long noses. They have long hair down their necks. This hair is called a mane.

Horses have long tails, too.
Their tails swing back and
forth all day.

Some male horses are called stallions. Other male horses are called geldings.

Female horses are called mares. A baby horse is called a foal.

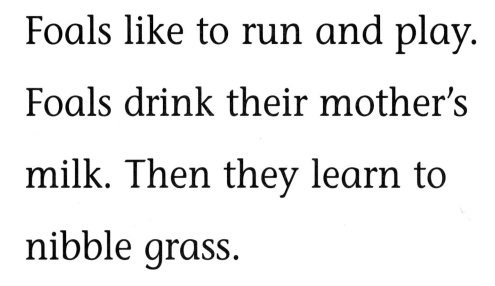

Foals like to run and play. Foals drink their mother's milk. Then they learn to nibble grass.

Horses eat many things. They eat oats, barley, and corn. Horses love to eat grass, too.

Horses like to live outdoors. They run and play in large fields called pastures. In cold weather, many horses live in barns.

Horses are smart and friendly animals. They are strong and can pull wagons and carts. Horses have been used for work for hundreds of years.

Many horses live just as pets. They are fun to ride and make good friends for people.

Index

barns, 16

foal, 11

food, 15

geldings, 8

manes, 4

mares, 11

milk, 12

pastures, 16

pets, 20

sounds, 3

stallions, 8

tails, 7

wagons, 19

work, 19

To Find Out More

Books

McDonald, Mary Ann. *Horses.* Chanhassen, Minn.: The Child's World, 1998.

Patent, Dorothy Hinshaw, and William Muñoz (photographer). *A Horse of a Different Color.* New York: Dodd, Mead, 1988.

Web Sites

Horse Country
http://www.horse-country.com/
A site that includes the Junior Riders Mailing Digest, the Horse Owners Club for Kids, and an international pen pal list for horse lovers.

Horse Fun
http://horsefun.com/index.html
Contests, puzzles, games, and more for the horse lover.

Note to Parents and Educators

Welcome to The Wonders of Reading™! These books provide text at three different levels for beginning readers to practice and strengthen their reading skills. Additionally, the use of nonfiction text provides readers the valuable opportunity to *read to learn*, not just to learn to read.

These leveled readers allow children to choose books at their level of reading confidence and performance. Level One books offer beginning readers simple language, word choice, and sentence structure as well as a word list. Level Two books feature slightly more difficult vocabulary, longer sentences, and longer total text. In the back of each Level Two book are an index and a list of books and Web sites for finding out more information. Level Three books continue to extend word choice and length of text. In the back of each Level Three book are a glossary, an index, and a list of books and Web sites for further research.

State and national standards in reading and language arts emphasize using nonfiction at all levels of reading development. The Wonders of Reading™ fill the historical void in nonfiction material for the primary grade readers with the additional benefit of a leveled text.

About the Authors

Cindy Klingel has worked as a high school English teacher and an elementary teacher. She is currently the curriculum director for a Minnesota school district. Writing children's books is another way for her to continue her passion for sharing the written word with children. Cindy Klingel is a frequent visitor to the children's section of bookstores and enjoys spending time with her many friends, family, and two daughters.

Bob Noyed started his career as a newspaper reporter. Since then, he has worked in communications and public relations for more than fourteen years for a Minnesota school district. He enjoys writing books for children and finds that it brings a different feeling of challenge and accomplishment from other writing projects. He is an avid reader who also enjoys music, theater, traveling, and spending time with his wife, son, and daughter.

Published by The Child's World®, Inc.
PO Box 326
Chanhassen, MN 55317-0326
800-599-READ
www.childsworld.com

Photo Credits
© Andre Jenny/Unicorn Stock Photos: 18
© Davis Barber/PhotoEdit: 2
© Dennis MacDonald/PhotoEdit: 9
© 1999 Dusty Perin/Dembinsky Photo Assoc. Inc.: 10
© Eascott/Momatiuk/Tony Stone Images: cover, 5
© Flanagan Publishing Services/Romie Flanagan: 6
© Fritz Prenzel/Tony Stone Images: 13
© 1993 Gijsbert van Frankenhuyzen/Dembinsky Photo Assoc. Inc.: 21
© Photri, Inc.: 14
© Rainer Grosskopf/Tony Stone Images: 17

Project Coordination: Editorial Directions, Inc.
Photo Research: Alice K. Flanagan

Library of Congress Cataloging-in-Publication Data
Klingel, Cynthia Fitterer.
Horses / by Cynthia Klingel and Robert B. Noyed.
p. cm. — (Wonder books)
Summary: A simple introduction to the physical characteristics and behavior of horses.
ISBN 1-56766-821-6 (alk. paper)
1. Horses—Juvenile literature.   [1. Horses.]
I. Noyed, Robert B.   II. Title.   III. Wonder books (Chanhassen, Minn.)

SF302 .K56   2000
636.1—dc21   99-057790

24

Horses.
Klingel, C.

PRICE: $20.13 (ONF/in/v)